DAY of THE DEPARTED

ADAPTED BY KATE HOWARD

W9-CAH-885

ISBN 978-1-338-11369-3

10 9 8 7 6 5 4 3 2 1   17 18 19 20 21
Printed in the U.S.A   40

First printing 2017

SCHOLASTIC INC.

THE HOLIDAY SPIRIT

"The Day of the Departed is my favorite holiday," sighed Nya, the Water Ninja. "I love all the lights!"

"And the costumes," said Kai, the Fire Ninja.

"And candy!" Jay, the Lightning Ninja, said through a mouthful of treats.

Master Wu nodded. "Yes, enjoy the fun and festivities. But never lose sight of the true meaning of the Day of the Departed." He smiled at Misako and the six ninja. "We light these lanterns to remember our ancestors. And to settle our debts."

"Ninja! Master Wu! Come!" cried Dr. Sander Saunders, the head of the Ninjago Museum of History. "Might I present our newest exhibit . . . the Hall of Villainy!"

The group walked into a room filled with statues of the most terrible villains the ninja had ever fought. "We have Samukai! Chen! Kozu! Cryptor! Morro! This exhibit is opening on the Day of Departed — and there is also a lunar eclipse."

Wu nodded. "The rarest Yin-Yang Eclipse."

"Scary holiday, scary exhibit, scary moon," Dr. Saunders said. "Magic is in the air!"

Cole, the Earth Ninja, read the card in front of Master Yang's portrait. "Yang will be remembered as the creator of Airjitzu." Cole shook his head. "*I* remember him as the guy who turned me into a ghost!" He looked down at a glowing blade inside a case. "Hey, Dr. Saunders, what's the story on this thing?"

But no one heard him. "Hello?" Cole called. Since he'd turned into a ghost, Cole often felt invisible. "It's like I don't exist anymore." He glared up at Master Yang's portrait. "And it's all your fault!"

THE DEPARTED

"The Yin Blade belonged to Master Yang," Dr. Saunders told the other ninja. "It is said to possess much Dark Magic. That's why it's sealed in this case made of ClearStone. No living being can get through it."

"*Cole . . .* " a voice called quietly. Master Yang's portrait began to glow. "Cole . . . *come*. Close the circle."

"Tell me you heard that," Cole said to his friends.

But the other ninja were gone.

"They don't even realize I'm gone," Cole grumbled. "Maybe *I'm* departed."

"If we never look to the past, we cannot see the future. On the Day of the Departed, we pause to remember those we've lost," Master Wu told the ninja.

Everyone scattered. Each had people to remember.

Zane used his ice powers to build an ice sculpture of his creator, Dr. Julien, in the forest.

Kai and Nya lit a lantern in honor of their parents.

Lloyd and Misako visited the statue of Garmadon.

Jay set off to spend the afternoon with his parents.

But Cole had a different plan for this Day of the Departed. He went to visit Master Yang in his haunted temple. Wu had said the Day of the Departed was a day for settling debts — and Cole and Yang had a serious debt to settle!

"All right, Yang," Cole called. He held up the Yin Blade he'd taken from the Ninjago Museum of History. "Show yourself!"

NIGHT OF THE RETURN?

"The Yin Blade!" Master Yang gasped. "What are you going to do?"

"There's magic in the air," Cole told him. "So I'm settling my debt!" He swung the Yin Blade at Yang.

Master Yang leaped to the side. The blade sliced through a stone orb as the moon entered its eclipse. Moonlight hit the orb, and bright green fog flowed out.

"You never should have played with Dark Magic, boy. This Day of the Departed will be remembered as my Night of the Return!" Yang cackled.

The green fog poured out of Yang's ghostly temple. The wind carried the fog into Ninjago City, where it flooded the Hall of Villainy. Suddenly, all the statues came to life!

"What has brought us back?" Master Chen asked.

"Perhaps *he* can explain," Morro said.

Yang spoke from his portrait on the wall. "My magic has brought you back from the Departed Realm. But you can only remain for the eclipse . . . unless you destroy the ninja who destroyed you. Do that, and you will take their places among the living.

"The ninja are spread around Ninjago," Yang told them. "You must each choose one and—"

"I call Zane!" yelled Samukai.

"The blacksmith's brats are mine!" called Chen.

"How come you get two?" asked Pythor, who just happened to be visiting the Hall of Villainy.

"Time is wasting," Yang snapped. "And I've got my own thing going on. So work it out!"

"Master Wu and I left things unfinished," said Morro. "I will settle our debt once and for all."

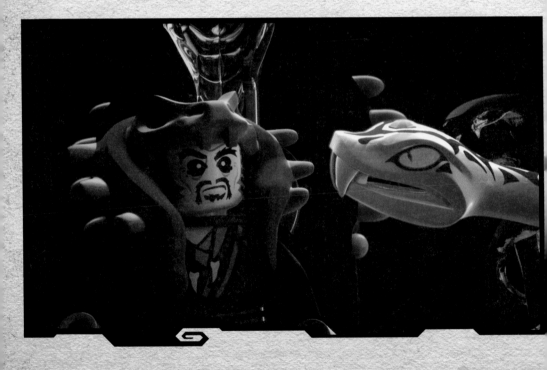

Back at Yang's temple, Cole was in trouble. "So . . . guys," he said to Yang's ghostly students, who were guarding him. "What say you help me out?"

"Your pleas are useless," Yang told him. "My students are loyal to no one but me."

"C'mon, guys!" Cole said, begging. "Yang is, like, the definition of evil."

Master Yang shook his head. "Actually, *Yang* means *good*. But I always did aspire for *great* . . ."

YANG'S CURSE

"I dedicated my life to the study of martial arts," Yang told him. "I mastered them all, and even created my own. Airjitzu was my first achievement, but it was nothing compared to finding the Yin Blade. The blade's magic is so powerful, it's said to hold the key to eternal life. But when I tested its powers on myself, something went . . . wrong."

Yang hung his head. "So while I will live forever, it is only as a ghost. Cursed to haunt this temple. Never able to return. Until tonight, thanks to you."

Yang smiled at Cole. "On the Day of the Departed, when there's a Yin-Yang Eclipse, the Yin Blade can cut the Rift of Return."

"You won't get away with this," Cole spat. "When my friends see I'm missing, they'll come for me!"

"See you're missing?" Yang snorted. "You can barely see yourself. Besides, you've caused a few problems for your friends . . . " He laughed gleefully. "There's no one to help you. Now excuse me . . . I have a rift to open."

Alone in his monastery, Wu sensed something was wrong. "An eclipse is always an omen," he said, looking up at the moon. "But is this one a sign of good or bad?"

Suddenly, Morro appeared behind him.

"Bad. *Very* bad," the Master of Wind whispered ominously.

All the ninja were in trouble.

When Nya and Kai stepped outside their parents' old blacksmith shop, they discovered one of their worst enemies had returned.

"Chen?!" Nya cried. "I don't know how you're here, but it's two against one."

"Is it?" Chen asked, giggling, as more villains appeared behind him.

Kai and Nya exchanged a look. This was not going to be an easy fight . . .

Meanwhile, Zane faced off against Cryptor and the Nindroids in the forest.

"Escape is futile, Zane," Cryptor growled. "You and I share programming. I know your every move before you even make it."

Zane smiled. He called on his friend Pixal, the android who shared his neural drive. Together, the pair tried to trick Cryptor, but they couldn't.

"Enjoy the Departed Realm," Cryptor said. "Oh, and say hi to dear old Dad!"

While Zane was trying to beat Cryptor, Jay was trying to protect his parents from the wrath of Samukai.

"I got this, Dad," Jay said, stepping forward. "Samukai, I have no idea what you want with my parents —"

Samukai cut him off. "It's not your parents I want, Jay. It's *you*!"

"Bring it!" Jay yelled. He pulled out his nunchuks and leaped into battle.

Back at Yang's temple, Cole raced through the hallways, searching for Yang. As he ran, he battled Yang's students one by one — until the only person left to stop was Yang himself.

Cole spotted the ghostly Master of Airjitzu at the top of a ladder. "I'm coming for you, Yang!" he called. "It's over. You don't have any more students to help you. You're all alone."

"I am not alone," Yang laughed as more students surrounded them. "Not at all."

Cole sighed. "Kinda wishing I wasn't alone, either . . ."

AN UNEXPECTED ALLY

Far from the temple, Wu faced off against Morro. "We have fought twice before. Though it pains me, I will do so again if I must."

Morro shook his head. "I'm not here to fight you," he told Wu. "I'm here to warn you. Master Yang has put your team in terrible danger. He has made you forget one of your own."

"Tell me more," Wu said.

"I will," Morro agreed. "But let's do it aboard the *Destiny's Bounty*. We have to warn the others."

Onboard the *Bounty*, Wu and Morro set off to alert the ninja. But the ninja were already busy battling their greatest enemies . . . and winning.

Outside their parents' old home, Nya and Kai climbed aboard Nya's speeder. Chen, Eyezore, and Zugu were hot on their trail.

"Duck!" Nya yelled to her brother as she raced under a tree. Though Chen and his partners were fierce, the brother and sister duo fought off all three villains!

"Can't . . . hold . . . on!" Lloyd grunted under the weight of a huge statue Pythor had used to trap him.

"You always underestimate me," Pythor taunted. "You're so like your father."

Misako nodded. "He's right, Lloyd. You're brave. And noble. And —"

Lloyd glanced up at the statue of his father, Garmadon, on the hillside above him. He took a deep breath. "And a master of Spinjitzu! You're still with me, Dad." Lloyd cast the statue off and spun toward Pythor. *"Ninjaaaaa-GO!"*

Deep in the forest, Zane had survived his fight with Cryptor and the Nindroids. But now Cryptor had Zane trapped, and there was nothing Pixal could do to help.

"It's no use fighting," Cryptor said. "I know your every move, Zane. And I know you never give up."

Zane had to fight differently if he wanted to win. He released his weapons. "Then I give up."

Cryptor swung his TechnoBlade at Zane, who leaped over it. The blade swung back at Cryptor, and he vanished in a puff of smoke. Zane and Pixal had won!

"This isn't personal, Jay," Samukai said, standing over Jay. "It's only so I can return to the living world. As soon as this is over, I'll release your parents."

"I'm on that!" yelled a voice from inside a huge mech. A metal arm pulled Jay's parents to safety.

"Ronin!" Jay whooped, spotting his friend inside the mech. "Thanks for coming to help."

"Uh, yeah . . . " Ronin said slowly. "I came to help. I definitely wasn't here to, um, 'borrow' some scrap metal for my mech while everyone was celebrating."

THE RIFT OPENS

Master Yang stood outside his temple, waiting to return to the living world.

"Yes! It is working!" Yang raised his Yin Blade toward the moon. "Close the circle . . . open the rift!"

The time was near. It wouldn't be long now . . .

Yang reached up his arms as the Rift of Return opened. "Freedom — it's all mine!"

But before Yang could fly through, Cole grabbed him. "No!" he cried.

Back in Ninjago City, the other ninja met up on the steps of the Ninjago Museum of History.

"Guys!" Jay panted. "I have the ghost story to end all ghost stories."

"Did you battle the possessed mannequin of a mortal enemy?" Kai guessed.

"Who tried to send you to the Departed Realm with magic blades?" Nya asked.

"But you defeated him first," Zane continued.

"And his ghost disappeared into the night," Lloyd said.

"So . . . yeah," Jay said, shrugging. "Why were all those ghosts out there?"

"Because distracting you was part of Master Yang's plan," Wu explained.

Morro floated over. "And Yang had help!"

When they saw Morro, the ninja all drew their weapons.

"Put away your weapons," Wu said. "Morro is here to help."

"Yang tricked Cole into helping him open a rift to return to the world," Morro explained.

The ninja looked around for Cole. Then they realized something: Cole wasn't there, and none of them had even noticed.

As the ninja and Wu raced to find their friend, Cole continued the fight against Master Yang.

"Just give up already," Yang told him.

"No!" screamed Cole. "I'm keeping you here until the eclipse ends and the rift closes. Your evil will never return."

Yang held up his Yin Blade. "What are you even fighting for? Your friends have abandoned you. Your Master has abandoned you. You are all alone!"

SETTLING A DEBT

Cole looked down at his hands. "I'm . . . fading away," he said sadly.

"Just one more lonely ghost," Yang laughed. "Not a friend in the world."

Just then, Cole heard a familiar voice.

"Cole!" It was Nya!

Cole spotted the *Destiny's Bounty* soaring through the sky. "My friends!"

At that moment, Cole's strength returned. He knocked Yang to the ground. "Ghost or not, I'm gonna do what I came here to do, Yang!

"You were wrong, Yang," Cole told him. "I'm not the one who's alone. You are!"

"No," Yang snapped, pointing to his students. "I have my family."

"No, you have prisoners. That's not family; that's captivity!" Cole said. Suddenly, his arms began to tingle. "I feel different . . . like I can punch through anything!" Cole cried, aiming another blow at Yang. The spell was broken.

"No!" Yang cried. One by one, his students shook off the spell that trapped them inside the temple.

"The rift!" Cole called to the students. "If you hurry, you can go through it and be free of this place forever!"

"I failed . . ." Yang moaned. "I always fail. I wanted to live forever, because I knew the day I was gone, no one would remember me."

"All of this was so you wouldn't be forgotten?" Cole asked him. "I get it. Believe me, I get it. I know what it's like to feel forgotten. It . . . hurts. But Master Yang, you *are* going to be remembered forever. You created Airjitzu!"

"Cole!" Kai screamed. "The rift! You gotta pass through the rift."

If Cole didn't go through the Rift of Return before it closed, he would remain a ghost forever.

"Come on," Cole said to Yang. "There's still time to go through. Both of us."

But Yang stopped. "The curse of the temple requires that at least one ghost remain behind as Master of the House." He grabbed Cole.

"What are you doing?" Cole screamed.

Master Yang smiled and threw him at the rift. "Settling my debt."

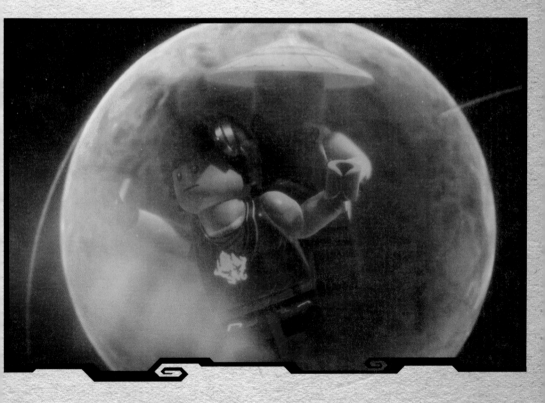

"Oh, no!" Jay wailed. "Cole is gone forever. I'd give anything to have him back."

"Anything?" Cole asked, stepping forward.

"Cole!" the ninja cried, running to hug their friend.

"You're not a ghost anymore," Lloyd said.

It was true. It had worked! Cole was human again.

"You look as good as new," Nya said.

"Thanks, Nya," Cole said, smiling at his friends. It was so good to be back with the team.